ready, steady, read!

Captain Daylight's Birthday Bash

Written and illustrated by
David Mostyn

Puffin Books

PUFFIN BOOKS

Published by the Penguin Group
Penguin Books Ltd, 27 Wrights Lane, London W8 5TZ, England
Penguin Books USA Inc., 375 Hudson Street, New York, New York 10014, USA
Penguin Books Australia Ltd, Ringwood, Victoria, Australia
Penguin Books Canada Ltd, 10 Alcorn Avenue, Toronto, Ontario, Canada M4V 3B2
Penguin Books (NZ) Ltd, 182–190 Wairau Road, Auckland 10, New Zealand

Penguin Books Ltd, Registered Offices: Harmondsworth, Middlesex, England

Published in Puffin Books 1996
10 9 8 7 6 5 4 3 2 1

Filmset in Monotype Bembo Schoolbook

Printed in England by Clays Ltd, St Ives plc

To Ruth

It was a warm summer morning.
Captain Daylight, the friendly
highwayman, opened his bedroom
window and looked out.

"Today is my birthday!" he said
to himself happily. "What a
wonderful day it's going to be."

Just the morning for a good gallop.

He jumped into his clothes and pushed a big flower into his button-hole. Then he went downstairs and opened the stable door. His horse, Buck, stretched out his head and sniffed the fresh, early morning air.

Captain Daylight rubbed his hands. Then he went indoors and sat down to breakfast.

"Knock knock. Who's there? Postman. Postman who? Postman with lots of birthday cards for you!" said Captain Daylight to himself.

He felt sure that the postman
would arrive at any minute with
lots of cards. But no one called.
The time for the delivery came
and went. Captain Daylight was
very disappointed.

No one's remembered my
birthday, he thought sadly. Oh
well, I shall just have to go for a
quiet ride by myself.

At that moment there was a loud
knock at the front door. Captain
Daylight jumped up.

"At last!" he cried. "That must be the postman. Better late than never!" But it wasn't the postman. It was a small boy called Albert Stiggins.

"Please, Captain," squeaked
Albert, "I've got a very important
message for you!"

"What is it, Albert?" asked
Captain Daylight.

"You're wanted in town," replied the boy. "Straight away."

"Who sent the message?" asked Captain Daylight.

"Joe," said Albert.

Joe was the driver of the local stagecoach. He was also Captain Daylight's best friend.

"He says you're to meet him at the Frog and Bulrushes Inn at twelve o'clock sharp."

"Right!" said Captain Daylight.
"Tell Joe I'll be there."

Albert tugged Captain
Daylight's sleeve.

Hang on a minute, Captain.

"What do you call a boy with a lump of earth on his head?" he asked.

Captain Daylight thought. "I don't know. What?"

"PETE!" yelled Albert, and ran off down the front path.

"Pete!" laughed Captain Daylight,
wiping his eyes. "He's a good lad,
that Albert."

Captain Daylight saddled up
Buck and galloped off to town.
No one had remembered his
birthday, but at least he could
enjoy a few jokes with his best
friend Joe. When Captain
Daylight got to the inn, Joe was
waiting for him at the door.

"What did the cannibal say after he'd been fishing?" Joe called out.

"No idea," shouted Captain Daylight.

"I haven't had a bite all day!"
shrieked Joe.

They both roared with laughter.

"Are you ready?" asked Joe.

"Ready for what?" said Captain
Daylight, suspecting another joke.

"Ready for your birthday party, that's what!" So saying, Joe flung open the door. There were all

Captain Daylight's friends waiting to wish him many happy returns of the day. Wally the shopkeeper shook his hand, and old Mrs Sharp gave him a brightly wrapped present. George and Mr Higgins slapped him on the back.

Everyone laughed and cracked jokes and ate birthday cake. The party was a huge success.

After a while, Joe the stagecoach driver stood up and called for silence. "I'm now going to ask Captain Daylight to make a speech," he said.

Captain Daylight jumped to his
feet. All his friends clapped and
cheered.

"Thank you all for this wonderful surprise party," he began. "Now I've got a surprise for you too. It's my newest and best summertime joke. How do you spell 'hungry horse' with only four letters?" But before anyone could answer, the door of the Frog and Bulrushes crashed open.

In strode a huge figure, dressed in black from head to toe. A deathly silence fell over the party-goers.

"Captain Daylight!" roared the
stranger.

"Y-yes?" quavered the Captain.

"Do you know who I am?"

"Y-you're B-black J-Jack M-M-
Midnight!"

"That's right!" snarled Black Jack.
"The greatest, fiercest highwayman
there is."

Black Jack glared at old Mrs
Sharp. Mrs Sharp fainted clean
away.

"What are you doing eating, drinking and cracking jokes with all these people? You should be robbing them!" he yelled.

Captain Daylight turned pale.

"You're a disgrace!" roared Black Jack. "You're making a laughing-stock of highwaymen everywhere. But *I'll* put a stop to that. I challenge you to a duel!"

Black Jack Midnight pulled out
two huge pistols and waved them
in the air. Captain Daylight's
knees began to shake.

"Pistols or fists?" roared Black Jack. "The choice is yours."

Captain Daylight was very frightened. He had only fired a pistol once in his whole life, and that had been an accident.

Black Jack Midnight grinned
horribly.

"Good," he growled. "I'll finish
you off in a few seconds, I will.
I'll pummel you, I'll pulverize you,
and I'll make your teeth rattle!"

Black Jack put his pistols away
and slowly stared round at
Captain Daylight's friends. Then
he sneered at the Captain.

"I'll make it easier for you," he said. "We'll have the fight in the stables. There's lots of soft hay for you to fall on." He roared with laughter and strode out of the room.

Gulp!

Captain Daylight followed him.

What's wobbly and shakes like a jelly? he thought to himself.

My knees! Oh my, I shouldn't be thinking of jokes at a moment like this.

All this time, Buck had been standing in the stable. He had enjoyed the gallop into town, but now he wanted to go home. It was very hot in the stable. The water – what little there was of it – wasn't fresh, and the hay tasted damp and musty.

Months past its sell-by date!
thought Buck.

He was getting into a very bad
temper indeed. All he wanted was
his nice, clean, cool stable at
home.

Suddenly the stable door was thrown open.

Aha! thought Buck. Here's
Captain Daylight. We can go
home now.

But to his great surprise he heard
a strange, loud voice behind him.
Then he felt himself being pushed
hard to one side.

"This'll do," bellowed Black Jack
Midnight, swaggering into the
stable. "I'll just throw out this
mangy old donkey, and then we
can begin."

Buck had had enough. He was feeling hot and tired and very hungry. Now, someone with a loud, rough voice had called him old and mangy and, worst of all, a DONKEY! Buck gathered all the strength that he had in his small body. He clenched his teeth and, with a great SNORT, he kicked out.

Black Jack had taken off his coat
and was just bending down to put
it on the ground, when Buck
kicked him right in the middle
of his huge bottom.

All Captain Daylight's friends had
gathered at the window to watch
the fight. They had seen the two
figures cross the yard and vanish

into the stables. For a moment
nothing happened. Everyone held
their breath.

Then, without warning, there was
a terrific yell and the huge figure
of Black Jack Midnight came
sailing out of the stable door. He
landed with a loud THUMP in
the middle of the yard.

53

"Good heavens!" shouted Joe.
"Captain Daylight's done it! He's
beaten Black Jack. Hooray!"

The stagecoach passengers made
a tremendous fuss of Captain
Daylight when he got back to
the inn.

"Have you read that book called *A Bump on the Head* by Esau Stars?" shouted Joe.

"No," laughed Captain Daylight, "but I've read one called *Catching Criminals* by Anne Ditover!"

Everyone roared with laughter.
They were proud of Captain
Daylight – he had saved the day.

"Let's get back to the party," said Captain Daylight. "Now, where was I? I was telling you my latest joke. How do you spell 'hungry horse' with only four letters? You give up? M-T-G-G!"

Everyone roared.

"Dear Captain Daylight,"
laughed old Mrs Sharp. "Such a
good joker, and after such a
terrific fight – not a hair out of
place."

The next day, when Buck was back in his cool, clean stable at home, Captain Daylight leaned over the stable door.

"I know it's just been *my* birthday," he said to Buck, "but I thought I'd get a special present for you, to thank you for all your help."

The present was a wonderful new bridle. It was made from soft black leather, and on each side of the headband was a small silver star.

"I chose the stars because you *are* a star," said Captain Daylight fondly, putting it on Buck.

Well, thought Buck, tossing his
head proudly, I'm going to get a
real kick out of wearing this!

ready, steady, read!

Other books in this series

Captain Daylight and the Big Hold-up
  David Mostyn

Cyril's Cat and the Big Surprise   *Shoo Rayner*

Cyril's Cat: Charlie's Night Out   *Shoo Rayner*

Farmer Jane   *Gillian Osband/Bobbie Spargo*

Farmer Jane's Birthday Treat
  Gillian Osband/Bobbie Spargo

The Hedgehogs and the Big Bag
  Vivian French/Chris Fisher

Hedgehogs Don't Eat Hamburgers
  Vivian French/Chris Fisher

The Little Blue Book of the *Marie Celeste*
  Angie Sage

The Little Green Book of the Last Lost Dinosaurs
  Angie Sage

The Little Pink Book of the Woolly Mammoth
  Angie Sage

The Get-away Hen
  Martin Waddell/Susie Jenkin-Pearce

The Lucky Duck Song   *Martin Waddell/Judy Brown*

Puffling in a Pickle   *Margaret Ryan/Trevor Dunton*

Swim, Sam, Swim   *Leon Rosselson/Anthony Lewis*